EB   Florian, Douglas.
            Turtle day

$12.89

DATE			
Diamond Bar 816			
JUN 1 8 1990			

Ri

L   816

TURTLE DAY

TURTLE DAY

BY DOUGLAS FLORIAN

Thomas Y. Crowell · New York

Turtle Day

Library of Congress Cataloging-in-Publication Data
Florian, Douglas.
   Turtle day / by Douglas Florian.
      p.   cm.
   Summary: Turtle's adventures include sunning on a log, going for
a swim, and being scared by a snake.
   ISBN 0-690-04743-6 : $
   ISBN 0-690-04745-2 (lib. bdg.) : $
   [1. Turtles—Fiction.]   I. Title.
PZ7.F6645Tu 1989   88-30321
[E]—dc19   CIP
                                                     AC

Typography by Carol Barr
1   2   3   4   5   6   7   8   9   10
First Edition

to my nephew, Raphael Lallouz

E arly in
the morning
Turtle woke up.

It was dark
inside his shell ...

so he stuck
his head out.

Turtle was cold . . .

so he sunned
on a log.

Turtle was hungry . . .

so he ate a
large leaf.

Turtle was thirsty . . .

so he drank
some cool water.

Turtle saw
his friend . . .

so they

played together . . .

and played
some more.

Turtle was hot . . .

so he went
for a swim.

Turtle saw
a big fish . . .

so he came

out of

the water.

Turtle was
scared by
a snake . . .

so he hid
in his shell.

It was late,
and Turtle
was very tired ...

so he slept

in his shell . . .

all night long.